It's
wintertime
once again!

Snowie is
excited to
meet new
friends!

He walked into the
woods until he
found the Squinny.

"Hello, Squinny! It's a
fine day to play in the
snow, " says Snowie to
Squinny the squirrel.
"Would you like to play
with me?"

"Sorry, I can't stay very
long in the cold," says
Squinny

There must be someone who can play with him in the snow.

"Hello, Foxer, it's a fine day to play in the snow, " says Snowie to the Foxer the fox. "Would you like to play with me?"

"Sorry, my feet gets very cold in the snow," says Foxer.

Snowie heard Piggie snorting.

"Hello, Piggie, it's a fine day to play in the snow, " says Snowie to the Piggie the pig. "Would you like to play with me?"

"Sorry, my body can't handle the cold, so I have to go back to the barn," says Piggie.

Snowie saw Ruben the Racoon coming over from a nearby tree.

"Hello, Ruben, it's a fine day to play in the snow, " says Snowie to Ruben. "Would you like to play with me?"

"Sorry, my fur gets wet, and I can't stand the cold," says Ruben.

Snowie saw Tina the
Tiger not too far
away.

"Hello, Tina, it's a fine
day to play in the
snow, " says Snowie to
Tina. "Would you like
to play with me?"

"Sorry, my paws will
freeze and slip into the
snow," says Tina.

Snowie saw Rex the Rabit running to get back to his hole.

"Hello, Rex, it's a fine day to play in the snow, " says Snowie to Rex. "Would you like to play with me?"

"Sorry, The snow gets too slippery, and I can't hop to play," says Rex.

Snowie saw Sweet the bird flying over at a distance.

"Hello, Sweet, it's a fine day to play in the snow, " says Snowie to Sweet. "Would you like to play with me?"

"Oh, my wings get too cold and I can't fly enough to play," says Sweet.

Sad and alone, Snowie thought this was going to be his first lonely winter.

"All my friends can't stay in the snow to play with me," says Snowie.

"Will I still be able to find a friend that will play with me in the snow?"

Then Snowie heard
someone laughing
and giggling.

"Hi! My name is Mico."

Covered in winter clothes, Mico was wearing boots, a scarf, mittens, and a cap.

"Would you like to play with me," asks Mico.

Snowie found a
new friend.

And together, they
enjoyed playing in
the snow.

www.B3autifullife.com

9 798371 533753